The Baby BOOM

'The Baby Boom'
An original concept by Jenny Moore
© Jenny Moore 2021

Illustrated by Gareth Williams

Published by MAVERICK ARTS PUBLISHING LTD
Studio 11, City Business Centre, 6 Brighton Road,
Horsham, West Sussex, RH13 5BB
© Maverick Arts Publishing Limited November 2021
+44 (0)1403 256941

A CIP catalogue record for this book is available at the British Library.

ISBN 978-1-84886-841-0

www.maverickbooks.co.uk

Brown

This book is rated as: Brown Band (Guided Reading)

The Baby BOOm

Written by
Jenny Moore

Illustrated by
Gareth Williams

Goo Goo GaGa!

Chapter 1

It was Saturday. At last! After a busy week at school, Will was looking forward to a whole weekend of fun. Today he was going skateboarding with his next-door neighbour, Suzy. Then tomorrow he was off fishing with Dad. He couldn't wait!

A dusty face emerged from the loft hatch as Will headed for the stairs. It was Mum. She was sorting out his old baby things to sell at the car boot sale the next day.

"Where are you going?" Mum asked, pulling a stray cobweb out of her hair.

"Skateboarding," said Will. "With Suzy."

Mum shook her head. "Oh no you're not. You're not going anywhere until you've sorted out your old toys for the car boot sale. I've asked you three times already."

Will sighed. He didn't want to be crawling round under his bed looking for old toy cars. He wanted to be outside doing slides and kickflips with Suzy.

"And what about your spellings for Monday?" asked Mum. "Have you finished learning them yet?"

Will sighed again. He hated spelling tests. Why did parents always spoil everyone's fun?

"Come on, love," said Mum. "I'm sure Suzy won't mind waiting. It shouldn't take you long, and then you'll have the whole weekend to enjoy yourself..." She stopped to listen. "Was that the letterbox? Can you go and check? I don't like going up and down this ladder all the time. It might be that book I ordered for Dad's birthday and I don't want him to see it."

Will trudged downstairs to have a look. But it wasn't a book, it was a free sample of something called Wonder Stuff.

"It looks like some kind of face cream," Will told Mum, holding it up to the hatch to show her. "There's a leaflet with it too, from someone called Madge Ick. *Would you like to look years younger?*" he read. "*Would you like smooth baby-soft skin? Then try new Wonder Stuff and prepare to be amazed.* And there's a money-off voucher for a full jar from her new shop in town."

"Oh," said Mum. She sounded disappointed. "Pop it in the bathroom and I'll have a look later. Thanks Will."

Chapter 2

Sorting out his old toys took Will much longer than he thought. He kept getting distracted by the old *Witch and Warlock* comics he found under his bed. It was almost 12 o'clock by the time he finished. Suzy would be wondering what had happened to him!

Mum had finished in the attic too. She was on the phone now, talking to her friend about the new Wonder Stuff cream.

"I just tried some," said Mum. "It's amazing! All the little lines round my eyes have vanished!

I'm going to pop down to Madge Ick's store after lunch and buy a full-sized jar of it... You should get some too. Trust me, you'll look years younger."

Will didn't see what was so great about being young. He couldn't *wait* to grow up. Grown-ups didn't have to do spellings. They got to see their friends whenever they wanted. And they didn't have parents telling them what to do all the time.

"Hey, where are you off to?" called Dad, as Will headed for the front door.

"Skateboarding with Suzy," said Will.

"No you're not," said Dad. "Not until you've had some lunch. I'm just about to make some cheese on toast."

Will put down his skateboard and trudged back towards the kitchen, wishing someone would invent a new Wonder Stuff cream for children. *Would you like to be older? Would you like to be grown-up and make your own rules? Then try new Wonder Stuff and prepare to be amazed.*

At last! Will was finally on his way to the skateboard park. He glanced in through the window of Madge Ick's store as he went past. The old lady behind the counter wasn't a very good advert for her cream. She was wearing strange, old-fashioned clothes and looked about a hundred years old! In fact she looked exactly like the witch from Will's *Witch and Warlock* comics. Her customers didn't seem to mind though. The queue stretched all the way down the street and round the corner. It seemed like *everyone's* parents wanted to look young again.

Chapter 3

Mum was still talking about the Wonder Stuff cream that evening. "I bet it's sold out by now," she said as they finished off their pudding. "They were selling so fast, I bought two jars in the end."

"That's good," said Dad. "I thought I might give it a try too. I've noticed a few wrinkles round my eyes lately." He winked at Will. "I want to look my best for our fishing trip tomorrow! In fact an early night might be a good idea too," he added with a yawn. "I want to be away as soon as it's light."

"Yes," agreed Mum. "And I want to be at the car boot sale as soon as it opens. Early nights for all of us, I think. Finish your pudding and then off to bed," she told Will.

Clear out your toys, thought Will as he headed upstairs. *Do your spellings. Eat your lunch. Go to bed.* Didn't parents *ever* get tired of telling their children what to do?

Will got into his pyjamas and curled up in bed with one of his old *Witch and Warlock* comics. He'd forgotten how good they were! He'd just finished a story about a backwards spell that reversed everything, when he remembered he hadn't brushed his teeth. But someone was already in the bathroom. It was Mum and Dad. They turned round and Will let out a snort of laughter.

Their faces were covered in thick green gloop!

"I'm just trying out that new cream of Mum's,"

said Dad, looking sheepish. "Would *you* like some?"

Will shook his head. "No," he said, still laughing.

"I'm young enough already, thank you."

Chapter 4

The sun shone brightly through Will's curtains the next morning. He stared at his alarm clock in confusion. Nine o'clock? What was going on? Dad had said he wanted to be away at the crack of dawn for their fishing trip. And what about Mum and her car boot sale? Why hadn't anyone come to wake him up?

There was no sign of Mum and Dad in the kitchen, and no sign of breakfast either. His parents must have overslept. That wasn't like them! He went up to their bedroom and peered round the door.

"What on earth...?" Will gaped at the sleeping figures on the bed, his mouth hanging open in shock. His mum and dad had vanished, leaving a pair of babies in their place! One of the babies was wearing space pyjamas, just like Dad's. And the other one was wearing owl pyjamas, just like Mum's. It was almost as if someone had shrunk his parents during the night, and made them young again.

Oh no, thought Will, remembering the Wonder Stuff cream. What if it had worked *too* well? What if it had made them look much, *much* younger? But that was impossible! Wasn't it?

"I must be dreaming," he said, pinching himself on the arm to try and wake himself up. "This *has* to be a dream."

Just then the doorbell rang. Will left the babies sleeping on the bed and hurried down to answer it. Suzy was waiting on the doorstep, clutching a baby to her chest.

"You've got to help me!" she wailed. "I tried calling Dad, but he didn't answer. He's away at a conference and it's the middle of the night there." Suzy took a big gulping breath. "This is going to sound really crazy," she said, "but I think this baby's my mum. I found her in Mum's bed this morning. She's even wearing Mum's pyjamas."

"The same thing happened to my parents," said Will. "It must be something to do with that Wonder Stuff cream they were using. Did your mum try it too?"

Suzy nodded. "She was hoping it would make her look younger. But not *this* young! What are we going to do?"

Chapter 5

A slow grin spread over Will's face. *What are we going to do?* That was an easy one!

"Whatever we want," he answered. "No grown-ups means no rules! We can have cake and ice cream for breakfast and spend the whole day on our skateboards. And then we can stay up all night watching television and playing computer games. It's brilliant!"

"No it's not," said Suzy. "It's terrible! If our parents are babies, that makes *us* the grown-ups.

We'll have to look after them now. And babies need a *lot* of looking after. A few hours helping out with my new baby cousin was enough for me!"

Will couldn't see what all the fuss was about. "Mine are sleeping peacefully," he said. "They're no trouble at all."

"But what about when they wake up and start screaming? What about when they want feeding? Or when they need their nappies changing?"

Nappy changes? Will gulped. He didn't like the sound of *that.*

There was a loud crying noise from upstairs, right on cue. *Two* loud crying noises.

"Oh no," said Will. He hurried up to his parents' bedroom to check on them, with Suzy following behind.

The babies were wide awake and screaming now, their arms and legs thrashing around wildly.

"What's wrong?" he asked, as Baby Dad sent his glasses flying across the room. "Are you hungry? Would you like some breakfast?"

Mum usually had muesli and Dad had toast, but those were no good for toothless babies.

The babies screamed harder.

"Are you thirsty? Would you like a drink?" Mum usually drank tea and Dad had coffee, but those were no good for babies either!

What else could it be? Maybe they were wet... or worse! Yuck! No, Will didn't want to think about *that*. "I know," he said. "How about a nice pram ride? We might not have any baby food or nappies, but we *do* have a pram."

"You do?" said Suzy.

"It used to be in the loft," said Will, raising his voice. It was hard to make himself heard over the screaming. "But Mum sorted all my old baby stuff out yesterday to sell at the car boot sale. It's in her van, ready to go. There's a baby sling there too. You can borrow that, if you like. And then maybe we should head down to the Wonder Stuff store and see if the owner knows how to turn our parents back into adults."

"Good idea," agreed Suzy. "Let's do it! I want my *old* mum back!"

Chapter 6

A small crowd of worried children and babies had

gathered round the Wonder Stuff shop. It looked

like the face cream had turned *everyone's*

parents young again.

But there was no sign of the owner, the mysterious Madge Ick. The shop was all locked up and abandoned. The sign above the door had gone and all the shelves were empty.

The flat above the shop looked empty too. There were no curtains in the windows and no one answered when the children rang the doorbell.

Will and Suzy went round the outside of the shop to see if there was another way in. Yes! The back door swung open on its hinges.

"Hello?" called Will. "Is anyone there?"

There was no answer.

The shop looked even more shut-up and abandoned on the inside. There was no sign of any more Wonder Cream, and no sign of Madge. *This is creepy*, thought Will, checking behind the counter for anything that might help them. He wished his proper grown-up parents were there to tell him what to do. He was starting to miss them.

"Aggh!" Will jumped as a hand grabbed his

shoulder. He span round in shock, but it was only Suzy!

"I've found something," she said. "It looks like a cauldron."

Will followed her, wheeling the pram. Suzy was right. It looked just like the cauldron in the *Witch and Warlock* comic strip he'd been reading the night before.

"There's something else here, too," Will cried, picking up the *Magical Creams and Potions* book lying beside it. "Madge Ick must be some kind of witch," he said, flicking through the tattered old pages. "And look, this must be the spell she used to make her Wonder Stuff. It's a recipe for 'Years-Off Youth Cream'. That *must* be it." He carried on flicking through the book. "But I can't find a spell to make people *older* though."

Suzy's mum began to whimper in her baby sling.

"Shh," said Suzy, jigging her up and down. "Don't worry Mum, we'll think of something."

"How about reversing the original spell?" Will suggested. "That's what they did in my comic. It's got to be worth a try."

Chapter 7

Will explained his plan to the other children. "All the ingredients in the original spell are to do with babies, like baby lotion, nappy cream, teething gel and baby dribble. But *we* need ingredients to do with old age. Things like toffees—my grandad *loves* toffees. And false teeth cleaning tablets."

"And tea," added Suzy. "The ladies at my great aunt's care home drink loads of tea."

"I can borrow some of my great grandma's perfume," someone said.

"And I can snip off some of my grandad's white hair while he's dozing," offered someone else. "He always has a little sleep after breakfast."

"Great!" said Will. "The more 'old' ingredients we have, the better. Let's get to work."

There were more children and babies arriving all the time. Everyone worked as a team, taking it in turns to fetch the ingredients and mind the crying parents. Will stirred the cauldron, hoping and praying that his idea would work. He *really* missed Mum and Dad now. *I need them to grow back up and start taking care of me again.*

"Alright," he said at last. "That should be enough now. Let's try the magic words...

Oldus Transformus!"

Nothing happened.

Will tried again, waving his fingers over the cauldron as he repeated the words, *"Oldus Transformus!"* Still nothing happened.

Will refused to give up though. It *had* to work. He thought for a moment. If this was a *reversing* spell, maybe he needed to reverse the magic words too. *"Sumrofsnart Sudlo!"* Will cried. The magical mixture bubbled and spat. It fizzed and frothed.

He leapt backwards as a flash of lightning hit the cauldron, lighting up the whole shop.

The mixture certainly *looked* the part now. But would it work?

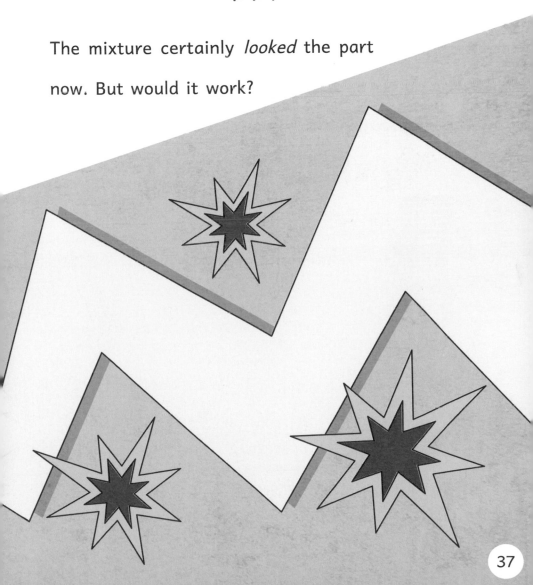

Will held his breath as he rubbed the cream onto his dad's nose and cheeks. Dad gurgled happily. He seemed to like it. Hopefully that was a good sign.

"It might need a bit of time to work," Will explained, as the other children did the same. The babies stopped crying and started gurgling instead. "Maybe we should take our parents back home while the spell's doing its magic."

Chapter 8

"Mum's getting really heavy," Suzy groaned as they turned into their road. "And she's much bigger than she was before."

"Same here," said Will, huffing and puffing as he pushed the pram along the pavement. His parents were fast asleep again now, but they were growing rapidly. "They're going to break the pram at this rate!"

He said a quick goodbye to Suzy at the front door and heaved his parents out of the pram. Will staggered up the stairs with them, one at a time, and settled them back down on their bed. Then he hurried off to the bathroom to hide the Wonder Stuff cream before it caused any more trouble. It was worth keeping though, just in case the new cream made his parents too old. He didn't want them ending up with false teeth and walking sticks!

But when Will got back to his parents' bedroom, they were their old selves again. *Thank goodness!*

Mum looked up sleepily as he came in. "Morning, love," she said. "Everything alright?"

"Yes," said Will. "It is now." He threw his arms round her. Mum hugged him back, then looked at the clock with a start. "Goodness me, is that the time? The car boot sale started hours ago. I must have slept right through the alarm."

Dad roused beside her. "Huh?" he grunted, looking confused. "How did it get so late? We'll have missed all the best spots for fishing." And then he grinned. "Never mind, how about cake and ice cream for breakfast instead, and then a trip to the skateboard park? You can teach us some new jumps," he added.

"Yes!" said Mum. "That would be awesome."

Will stared at them in surprise. Maybe there was still a *bit* of young magic left in them after all!

The skateboard park was filled with mums and dads falling off their children's boards and being generally embarrassing. But the children didn't care. They were just pleased to have their parents back. And no one was more pleased than Will.

Even when the last of the magic wore off and Mum started talking about spellings and tidying up, Will didn't mind. He didn't mind when Dad suggested picking up some extra vegetables on their way home to make up for their sugary breakfast. Things were finally back to normal and he couldn't be happier.

"That's strange," said Mum as they passed the Wonder Stuff store. "It looks like it's closed down. Mind you," she added, "that cream wasn't much good after all. I've still got those lines round my eyes."

"Me too," said Dad.

"Good," Will told them. "I love every one of those lines. You shouldn't wish them away. You're perfect, just as you are."

Discussion Points

1. Where was Will trying to go at the beginning of the story?

2. What made Will's parents turn into babies?
a) A magical machine
b) A super sweet milkshake
c) An anti-aging cream

3. What was your favourite part of the story?

4. How did Will and the other kids turn their parents back into adults?

5. Why do you think the parents all wanted to go to the skate park after they changed back?

6. Who was your favourite character and why?

7. There were moments in the story when Will had to be **responsible**. Where do you think the story shows this most?

8. What do you think happens after the end of the story?

Book Bands for Guided Reading

The Institute of Education book banding system is a scale of colours that reflects the various levels of reading difficulty. The bands are assigned by taking into account the content, the language style, the layout and phonics. Word, phrase and sentence level work is also taken into consideration.

The Maverick Readers Scheme is a bright, attractive range of books covering the pink to grey bands. All of these books have been book banded for guided reading to the industry standard and edited by a leading educational consultant.

To view the whole Maverick Readers scheme, visit our website at

www.maverickearlyreaders.com

Or scan the QR code to view our scheme instantly!

Maverick Chapter Readers
(From Lime to Grey Band)